Dear Parent:
Your child's love of reading starts here!

Every child learns to read in a different way and at his or her own speed. Some go back and forth between reading levels and read favorite books again and again. Others read through each level in order. You can help your young reader improve and become more confident by encouraging his or her own interests and abilities. From books your child reads with you to the first books he or she reads alone, there are I Can Read Books for every stage of reading:

SHARED READING
Basic language, word repetition, and whimsical illustrations, ideal for sharing with your emergent reader

BEGINNING READING
Short sentences, familiar words, and simple concepts for children eager to read on their own

READING WITH HELP
Engaging stories, longer sentences, and language play for developing readers

READING ALONE
Complex plots, challenging vocabulary, and high-interest topics for the independent reader

ADVANCED READING
Short paragraphs, chapters, and exciting themes for the perfect bridge to chapter books

I Can Read Books have introduced children to the joy of reading since 1957. Featuring award-winning authors and illustrators and a fabulous cast of beloved characters, I Can Read Books set the standard for beginning readers.

A lifetime of discovery begins with the magical words "I Can Read!"

Visit www.icanread.com for information
on enriching your child's reading experience.

Also available

Dumpy's Apple Shop

Dumpy to the Rescue

Dumpy's Extra-Busy Day

Dumpy's Valentine Copyright © 2006 by Dumpy, LLC All rights reserved. No part of this book may be used or reproduced in any manner whatsoever without written permission except in the case of brief quotations embodied in critical articles and reviews. Printed in the United States of America. For information address HarperCollins Children's Books, a division of HarperCollins Publishers, 1350 Avenue of the Americas, New York, NY 10019. www.harperchildrens.com

Library of Congress Cataloging-in-Publication Data

Edwards, Julie, date
   Dumpy's valentine / by Julie Andrews Edwards and Emma Walton Hamilton ; illustrated by Tony Walton with Katie Boyd.— 1st ed.
   p.   cm.— (My first I can read book) (The Julie Andrews collection)
   Summary: Dumpy the Dump Truck delivers valentines when the mail truck breaks down on Valentine's Day.
   ISBN-10: 0-06-088573-4 (trade bdg.) — ISBN-13: 978-0-06-088573-1 (trade bdg.)
   ISBN-10: 0-06-088575-0 (pbk.) — ISBN-13: 978-0-06-088575-5 (pbk.)
   [1. Valentine's Day—Fiction. 2. Valentines—Fiction. 3. Dump trucks—Fiction. 4. Trucks—Fiction.] I. Hamilton, Emma Walton.
II. Walton, Tony, date, ill. III. Title. IV. Series. V. Series: The Julie Andrews collection
PZ7.E2562Dy 2005   2005017797
[E]—dc22   CIP
                                                                                                         AC

1 2 3 4 5 6 7 8 9 10 ❖ First Edition

Tony Walton and Katie Boyd warmly thank Ruby Randig

Dumpy's
Valentine

By Julie Andrews Edwards and Emma Walton Hamilton
Illustrated by Tony Walton
with Katie Boyd

HarperCollins*Publishers*

Hooray! It's Valentine's Day!
Pop-Up and Charlie
are driving to town.

Oh dear!
Trusty the Mail Truck
has broken down!
Who will deliver
the valentine cards?
Toot! Toot! Dumpy can help!

Here's one
for the flower shop!
Toot! Toot!

But what's this? A rose!

Thank you!

Happy Valentine's Day!

Here's one
for the candy store!
Toot! Toot!
But what's that?

A box of chocolates!

Thank you!

Happy Valentine's Day!

Here's one for the paper shop!
Toot! Toot!

But what's this? Stickers!

Thank you!

Happy Valentine's Day!

Here's one for the firehouse!
Toot! Toot!

But what's this? A gold star!

Thank you!

Happy Valentine's Day!

Here's one for the lighthouse!
Toot! Toot!

But what's this? Seashells!
Thank you!
Happy Valentine's Day!

Look how many
for the schoolhouse!

Toot! Toot!

Happy Valentine's Day!

But what about poor Trusty?

We have a rose,

a box of chocolates, stickers,

a gold star, seashells,

and *lots* of stamps.

Let's make

a *big* valentine for him!

Toot! Toot!

Happy Valentine's Day,
Trusty!

And Happy Valentine's Day,
Dumpy!
We love you!